UNIPIGGLE
The Unicorn Pig!

She's a mud princess

He's a muddy unicorn pig

Together, they're a PERFECT match!

For Martha and Winona –
reading superstars!

First published in the UK in 2022 by Usborne Publishing Ltd., Usborne House,
83-85 Saffron Hill, London EC1N 8RT, England, usborne.com

Usborne Verlag, Usborne Publishing Ltd., Prüfeninger Str. 20,
93049 Regensburg, Deutschland VK Nr. 17560

Text and illustrations copyright © Hannah Shaw, 2022

This is a work of fiction. The characters, incidents, and dialogues are products of the author's
imagination and are not to be construed as real. Any resemblance to actual events or persons,
living or dead, is entirely coincidental.

A CIP catalogue record for this book is available from the British Library.

ISBN 9781801316736   07708/1   JFMAMJ ASOND/22

Printed in UAE.

MIX
Paper | Supporting
responsible forestry
FSC® C004800
www.fsc.org

Fairy
Freeze

HANNAH SHAW

USBORNE

Twinkleland Palace & gardens

Hidden cove

Better Land

The Harbour

Twinkletown

Village of Fancy Pants

Bug Island

Dragonton Cave complex

Volcano Lake

WELCOME TO

This is Princess Peony Peachykins Primrose
Pollyanna Posh, usually known as Princess Pea.
She lives in Twinkleland Palace with her parents,
Queen Bee and King Barry.

She likes: mud, marshmallows, chocolate and
having fun.

TWINKLELAND!

This is Unipiggle. He's Princess Pea's Royal Companion. He's a loud, muddy and proud unicorn pig.

He likes: mud, marshmallows, chocolate, having fun and getting tickled behind the ears.

Princess Pea was supposed to choose a **UNICORN** as her Royal Companion. But during the Unicorn Parade, there was a **STORM** and things went a bit **WRONG**. Luckily, Unipiggle saved the Princess and the day.

Now, Princess Pea and Unipiggle love going on lots of adventures together. (It was fortunate that Princess Pea didn't get a real unicorn, because they need constant praise.)

1

Let it Snow!

"Unipiggle, come quick! It's **SNOWING**!"

Princess Pea was twirling around on
her balcony in her pyjamas. A blanket
of soft, pillowy white snow had covered
Twinkleland and the palace gardens
overnight. A rare snowbow glimmered
over the distant mountains. It only
snowed for a day or two once a year
in Twinkleland, so this was
very exciting!

Unipiggle grunted eagerly and wriggled out from under the cosy royal duvet. He trotted over to the open doors and was delighted to feel an icy snowflake land on the end of his snout.

Princess Pea rushed back inside and pulled on her favourite yellow wellies. "Let's go out straight away!"

Unipiggle didn't need to be told twice. This was his first winter in Twinkleland and the snow looked like so much fun! They bolted out of the bedroom door together and skidded down the perfectly polished marble corridor towards the grand staircase.

"Ahem!" Queen Bee stepped out into the hallway.

Screeeeech!

Unipiggle and Princess Pea skidded to a halt.

"And where do you think you are going?" the Queen asked them, putting her hands on her hips and raising a stern eyebrow.

"It's snowing, Mummy! We were just heading out…"

"My goodness!" tutted the Queen. "You cannot possibly go out without a cloak, a hat and scarf, mittens, two pairs of socks and a healthy breakfast!" She eyed Unipiggle. "And I have just the thing to keep *you* toasty!"

After getting dressed, Princess Pea and Unipiggle reluctantly sat down at the breakfast table and nibbled at some cress-flavoured jam on soggy toast (unfortunately, the Queen was overkeen on putting salad in everything). Without warning, the Wardrobe Pixies pounced with an assortment of knitted garments.

"I can't see!" complained Princess Pea, peering out from under her bobble hat.

"OINK!" Unipiggle protested loudly as two pixies wrangled him into one of the King's old jumpers that he certainly didn't need to wear. His dried-on mud kept him warm.

A Post Pixie hurried past with a teetering pile of silver envelopes.

"I want those invitations delivered quickly. The **Very Important Guests** must know that the Twinkleland Palace Snow Ball will take place tomorrow!" the Queen called after them.

Unipiggle and Princess Pea exchanged gleeful glances. They'd been looking forward to the Snow Ball ever since Queen Bee and King Barry had announced that this winter they would celebrate the seasonal snowfall with a **BIG** party.

There hadn't been a Snow Ball at the palace since Princess Pea was a baby, because the Queen was very fussy about mess, and throwing a party meant lots of guests would be trampling all over the palace and gardens. However, the King had recently pointed out that a Snow Ball was unlikely to make as much of a mess as a **herd of muddy unicorns**,

a rampaging dinosaur

or even **giant exploding pumpkins** (but of course, those are other stories).

The Queen had agreed. She was now determined to make the Snow Ball a very special occasion, and she'd even asked Princess Pea and Unipiggle for ideas. Unipiggle couldn't wait to tuck into a yummy festive banquet and Princess Pea wanted to see the palace come alive with sparkle and cheery partying.

The Queen inspected her exceedingly long list. "I've put in an enormous order of decorations, lights and gifts with the **Festive Fairies**. Everything should arrive this morning. I want it all to be **PERFECT**!"

Princess Pea had already told Unipiggle all about the Festive Fairies. There was a whole chapter about them in her favourite book, *The Magical Creature Guide*.

Festive ✳ ✳ Fairies

The Festive Fairies ride sleighs pulled by flying reindeer and deliver festive cheer, gifts, lights and decorations to all of Twinkleland every year when it snows. They have an underground workshop in a secret location.

"I do hope we'll catch a glimpse of them today, Unipiggle! I've never seen them. They always come and leave so quickly when they deliver gifts...but this year, with the extra decorations for the Snow Ball, surely it will take them a while to unload their sleighs?"

Unipiggle's eyes lit up. He wanted to see the flying reindeer.

The Queen studied her list again. "Where is King Barry when I need him?"

She sighed and marched off to the kitchens. Princess Pea smiled. The only advantage of her mummy being so busy was that she'd forgotten to give Princess Pea her usual Perfect Princess schedule for the day.

Unipiggle had already headed to the door and was oinking to be let out.

"Okay, Unipiggle, let's go play in the snow!"

Snow Piggle

Unipiggle **LOVED** the snow. He frolicked around while Princess Pea stomped happily. She was satisfied to find the snow was nice and deep, but not quite deep enough to go over the tops of her wellies.

We can see out too!

Unipiggle jumped into a snowdrift. It was soft, cold and refreshing. Then Princess Pea and Unipiggle headed to the First Best Lawn together. It was time to get creative!

They started to shovel snow into a large pile. As a form began to take shape, Princess Pea found some pebbles for eyes and a stick for the mouth.

"Who is that supposed to be?" asked a familiar voice. It was their friend, Arthur the Gardener Pixie.

"Hi, Arthur! Do you want to make a snow pixie?" Princess Pea asked.

Arthur sniffed. His nose and pointy ears were pink with cold and his teeth were chattering. "I…I…I'm not sure…I understand…what is quite s…s…so fun…about snow!" he complained, shivering in his boots.

Princess Pea took off her cosy bobble hat and offered it to Arthur, who pulled it on top of his own hat. Unipiggle wiggled out of the silly jumper he'd been forced to wear and gave it to Arthur as well. It was rather large for the pixie, but Unipiggle was just pleased to get rid of it.

"Ah, that's better!" Arthur smiled. "But I really can't stop, I need to prepare the gardens for the Snow Ball. As soon as the Festive Fairies deliver the ice sculptures and fairy lights, I'll have to decorate all the trees."

"Unipiggle and I can help you with that!" Princess Pea offered and Unipiggle nodded enthusiastically. Decorating trees and hanging out lights didn't sound like a chore at all. "Just let us know when they arrive."

As Arthur crunched back along the path to his warm shed, Unipiggle and Princess Pea headed off to the Second Best Garden to see the swimming pool, enjoying making big footsteps in the snow as they went. It wasn't that they wanted to go for a swim (it was far too chilly for that!), but they wanted to see whether the pool was frozen or not.

"Ahoy there, Peasprout and Piggykins!" called King Barry. "Isn't it wonderful? We have an **ICE RINK**! The pool is completely frozen solid — I've already tested it."

Princess Pea and Unipiggle were impressed.

"I'm practising my skating for the Snow Ball tomorrow. Watch and learn!" boasted the King. They stood and watched as King Barry tightened his skates, smoothed down his cherished purple moustache, puffed out his chest and then stepped confidently onto the ice…

SLIP!

The King lost his balance almost immediately. He flapped his arms around in a desperate attempt to stay upright.

BUMP!

He landed hard on his bottom.

Unipiggle looked amused and Princess Pea smothered a giggle as two pixies zoomed over to the King and helped him stand up again.

Teehee!

"Oh yes, it's super easy!" the King bluffed, wobbling around the rink with the two pixies holding him upright. "Why don't you try?" King Barry beckoned them onto the ice. "There's a box of ice skates there. I found them in the attic and thought it would be fun!"

Unipiggle was not convinced that slippery surfaces were the natural habitat of unicorn pigs. If King Barry's performance was anything to go by, he felt much happier standing at the edge to watch.

But Princess Pea had already found a pair of skates that fitted and was soon shuffling around on the ice, encouraging him to join her.

Unipiggle took a deep breath and bravely put one trotter onto the rink, then another…

Without moving at all, he started to **slide**…
and **slip** and **spin**!

"Oh, Unipiggle!" Princess Pea clapped.
"You're doing it!"

Unipiggle quickly decided he did **NOT** like
ice skating. He wanted to get off the ice, but the
faster he moved his trotters, the more he spun!

33

Yikes! Unipiggle **whizzed** across the rink and **CRASHED** into King Barry and his poor skating pixies.

As Princess Pea helped everyone to their feet, a pixie rang the bell for lunch. Unipiggle was very relieved indeed.

They squelched back to the Grand Hall, where a tureen of vegetable soup had been put out for them. The Queen hadn't sat down to eat though; she was pacing around, looking at her watch.

Princess Pea and Unipiggle noticed there were no decorations up yet, no lights, no gifts. The Palace Pixies were cleaning the floors and the windows, but they looked anxious.

Queen Bee let out a loud sigh. "The Festive Fairies haven't been yet. How can we prepare for the Snow Ball?"

King Barry hobbled in and helped himself to a steaming bowl of soup. "Oh, don't you worry, Bee darling. Those fairies have to deliver to all of Twinkleland first! I expect they're just down the hill, bringing cheer to Twinkletown as we speak!"

"I wish they'd hurry!" Queen Bee frowned.

Princess Pea and Unipiggle slurped down their soup and joined the pixies staring expectantly out of the window. It had stopped snowing and everything seemed quiet and still outside.

"I have a brilliant idea, Unipiggle!" hissed Princess Pea. "Instead of staying here and waiting, we could go and *find* the Festive Fairies! We could offer to help them and show them the way to the palace in case they've forgotten!"

Unipiggle grinned. It was time for a snowy adventure!

Missing Sparkle

"Are you ready, Unipiggle? This will definitely be the quickest way to get down the hill!" yelled Princess Pea. She was sitting on a wooden sledge they'd found in one of the stables. It was very old, but it still looked like it would carry them.

Before they'd headed out of the palace, Princess Pea had left a note to tell her parents what she was doing:

We have gone to find the Festive Fairies — ♛ Pea & Unipiggle

Then she packed her satchel with a warm drink and a few pies pinched from the palace kitchen. Unipiggle had already used his magic to turn the celery pies into chocolate while the Pixie Chef's back was turned. (Most magic was banned in Twinkleland because it was too messy and unpredictable, but Unipiggle often "forgot" that rule!)

Now they were outside the palace gates at the top of the hill, looking down at Twinkletown below. Unipiggle eyed the sledge with some suspicion, but he sat his bottom squarely on the back, behind Princess Pea. This action set the sledge moving — it creaked over the snow, slowly at first. But as the hill steepened, the sledge began to go faster and faster, until they were hurtling down at breakneck speed...

Halfway down, the sledge overturned and Princess Pea fell off! She tumbled into the soft snow. Unipiggle fell off soon after, along with more bits of the sledge. Unlike Princess Pea, he didn't stop. He rolled head over trotters the rest of the way down the hill, gathering snow as he went.

Eventually, he rolled to a halt at the bottom.

"You look like a giant snowball," chuckled Princess Pea, as she shook off the snow and retrieved the sledge.

Unipiggle blew snow out of his snout and wiggled his tail and they headed on into Twinkletown.

"Your Highness! Royal Piggy!" Twinklefolk waved to them as they dragged the old sledge through town. But things didn't look twinkly or fun in Twinkletown either. Here, like in Twinkleland Palace, there were no lights or decorations. Instead, everyone looked chilly and fed up.

Mummy, when will the Festive Fairies come?

Twinkletown was missing its festive sparkle.

Princess Pea and Unipiggle stopped outside the bakery, home to Baker Troll and his fluffy pet cat. Baker Troll was famous for his delicious many-tiered cakes. However, instead of a cheerful festive display, the cake shop looked drab and empty.

SORRY!
NO CAKES

"Sorry! There are no cakes today," Baker Troll said. "I ordered a box of celebration-cake ingredients, decorations and even special fairy-cake cases from the Festive Fairies, but nothing has arrived! And the Queen asked me to bring cakes to the Snow Ball at the palace tomorrow. What can I do?"

Unipiggle grunted in sympathy (he was also disappointed there was no cake). The baker's cat mewed sadly.

"That's strange," said Princess Pea thoughtfully. "The Festive Fairies haven't been to the palace yet either! We thought they might have got lost down here. Where can they be?"

Baker Troll's eyes lit up. He'd remembered something. "Could they be in the village of Fancy

Pants? The villagers usually order new pants from them every winter! Maybe the fairies are still busy delivering **LOTS** of new pants?"

Princess Pea and Unipiggle chuckled.

"Don't worry, Baker Troll," Princess Pea reassured him. "The Festive Fairies will come to Twinkletown and the palace; there will be cake! Unipiggle and I are going to find out where they've got to."

Princess Pea and Unipiggle waved goodbye to the baker and his cat and set off again on the road that led to the village of Fancy Pants.

"Giddy up, Unipiggle, I can see Fancy Pants ahead! We have an urgent mission to find the Festive Fairies and save the Snow Ball!"

Old Pants

"Greetings! Have you come with news?" The Mayor of Fancy Pants plodded out to meet Unipiggle and Princess Pea and pulled their sledge up the little hill to the village. The Mayor was wearing enormous, billowing bloomers, and had two tennis rackets strapped to his feet to help him walk in the snow. He welcomed them into the village hall. "Come on in and warm up!"

A large group of villagers, all of whom were wearing their well-worn fancy pants, followed them in. They were eager for news too.

"The Festive Fairies bring new pants for us every year," the Mayor explained. "Our old pants have almost worn through now. They're not nearly as fancy as they used to be and some of us have had to patch ours!" He pointed to his bottom. "What will we wear to the Snow Ball if there are no new pants?"

Princess Pea tried not to laugh. "I'm sorry, we haven't seen the Festive Fairies, but we've been searching for them."

"Look! The snow has already started to melt in the sunshine!" cried a villager, pointing to a muddy puddle that was quickly forming outside the door. "The Festive Fairies only come when there is snow." He sniffed. "What if...they don't come at all now?"

Everyone in the room gasped. Unipiggle oinked in dismay (although the muddy puddle did look tempting to jump in). Princess Pea felt a little panicked that the snow was melting. She hadn't noticed that the sun had come out. What if it didn't snow again? Would the Snow Ball be cancelled altogether?

She took a deep breath and turned to the Mayor of Fancy Pants. "Unipiggle and I want to make sure that the Snow Ball goes ahead too! We are trying our best to work out what's happened and where the Festive Fairies have got to…" Just then, she was struck by another worrying thought. Not wanting to alarm the villagers further, she turned to Unipiggle and whispered, "*If they aren't here, and they aren't in*

Twinkletown or at the palace, maybe something
has gone wrong at their festive workshop!"

Unipiggle's eyes grew wide. Of course!
That was where they needed to head next.

"We will visit the Festive Fairy workshop!"
Princess Pea declared confidently to everyone.

"Wherever that is…"

"I can take you

there!" piped up

a tiny voice.

Unipiggle turned
his head and
blinked as a fairy
wearing tiny
sparkly fancy pants
introduced herself.

"I'm Nora. I'm not a Festive Fairy but my cousin Bertie is. I also write stories for the *Twinkleland Times*, and joining you on this little adventure would make a great article!"

"We'd be grateful for your help!" Princess Pea told Nora. "But we must leave immediately. We need to solve the mystery of the missing fairies before the snow melts!"

"Fantastic plan!" The Mayor applauded, looking somewhat relieved.

As they were cheered off, Unipiggle smiled to himself and thought about the magic he'd secretly performed in the village hall when no one was looking. The villagers would have some delicious chocolate pants to munch on as they waited for the Festive Fairies to arrive.

"The Festive Fairy workshop is hidden in the Fairy Well Dell and the quickest route there is down the river on the ice," Nora informed them as they bumped along on the sledge.

Unipiggle shook his head when he heard the word "ICE". He wasn't going on ice again!

"Come on, Unipiggle, we have no choice. We have to do it if we want to save the Snow Ball!" Princess Pea coaxed him. "Look, there's the river ahead!"

Staring out at the meandering frozen river, they could see it was starting to look a little thin and melty in places. Princess Pea gulped. She suddenly felt less sure herself.

Unipiggle's trotters trembled as he pushed the sledge off the bank then launched himself onto it; thankfully the ice seemed solid enough. Princess Pea leaped on too and Nora flew over and clung to his horn. Unipiggle squeezed his eyes tightly shut as they started to slide...

They were off!

Creak! Ping! Crack!

As they hurtled down the river, even more bits of the sledge flew off behind them.

When they finally stopped spinning, Unipiggle opened his eyes again. They were teetering on the brink of a frozen waterfall!

They all squealed and scrambled off the sledge. Then they watched in horror as the sledge tipped forward and toppled off the edge of the waterfall. It splintered into pieces on the icy rocks below. Unipiggle shuddered, but the movement made him wobble. He was sliding towards the edge too!

"Oh no!" Princess Pea shrieked. She and Nora quickly grabbed hold of Unipiggle by his curly tail and helped pull him to the safety of the riverbank.

"Oops! I forgot all about the dangerous waterfall!" said Nora breathlessly. "Luckily the Festive Fairy workshop is only a short walk from here." She took the opportunity to scribble down notes in her notebook while Unipiggle and Princess Pea spent a few moments recovering with a chocolate pie and a warm drink.

Then they picked themselves up and dusted themselves off. Unipiggle looked determined as they set off on foot. They were one snowy step closer to finding out just what had happened to the Festive Fairies…

Fairy Well Dell

"Here we are!"

"Ooh!" breathed Princess Pea as they stepped into a wooded glade. Unipiggle gazed around their new surroundings. They had never been to this part of Twinkleland before. Frost-dusted trees with stripy candy canes hanging from their branches surrounded a sweet little wishing well, while a beautiful snowbow shimmered above them. Unipiggle felt like there was definitely magic in the air.

Princess Pea looked thoughtful. "My book, *The Magical Creature Guide*, said the secret Festive Fairy workshop was underground somewhere. How do we find the entrance?" They really did need to hurry up as the afternoon sun was making more of the snow thaw.

Nora pointed to the well. "I *think* that's the way down… Cousin Bertie always meets me up here in the glade, so I've never actually been down there myself!"

Unipiggle peered into the wishing well. It was empty of water. He felt another tingle of magic and gave an enthusiastic oink.

"But we're not small enough to fit down there!" Princess Pea laughed. "Unipiggle will definitely get stuck!"

Unipiggle nodded sadly. There had been quite a few bumps and scrapes on this adventure already and he didn't fancy getting stuck in a well too.

Nora giggled. "There's an easy way to solve that problem!" She flew over to a tree and picked two candy canes. "Try eating these!"

Unipiggle loved sweets, so he licked his lips and greedily gulped down a candy cane without a second thought.

Princess Pea blinked and looked down at her feet. *Unipiggle was now the size of one of her wellingtons!*

"Oink oink!" he squeaked in shock.

"My goodness, Unipiggle! You're tiny and so cute!" Princess Pea bent over to tickle him.

"I guess these are magic shrinking canes?"
The Princess studied her candy cane then
cautiously took a bite. A funny sinking sensation
rippled through her body and by the time she'd
finished munching, she was staring up at a
HUGE well.

"Don't worry, you won't stay like that forever. It will wear off at some point!" said Nora, getting out her notebook again and scribbling something down.

Princess Pea and Unipiggle walked around the wishing well. They'd noticed a hole just big enough to crawl through. When they peered through the gap, they saw it led to a spiralling slide.

"This must be the way!" Princess Pea called to Nora. They were so close to finding the fairies now and Princess Pea felt increasingly hopeful the Snow Ball could be saved.

Unipiggle bravely volunteered to go first. He hurtled down the slide, followed closely by Princess Pea and Nora.

They shot out of the end and landed at the bottom of the well on a carefully placed feathery mattress.

FLUMPF!

Nora switched on her fairy wand, illuminating two passages ahead. Everything smelled damp and earthy. One of the passages looked like a rabbit hole, while the other was closed off by a door with a polished door knocker and a little silver bell.

Unipiggle trotted over to the door and gave it a push with his snout. It was locked.

"You're right, Unipiggle! The Festive Fairy workshop must be **BEHIND** that door!" said Princess Pea excitedly.

"Try ringing the bell?" suggested Nora.

Unipiggle tried pulling on the bell cord.

Ting-a-ling-a-ling!

They waited and listened. But they couldn't hear anyone coming.

Unipiggle frowned and pulled the bell again.

Ting-a-ling! Ting-a-ling-a-ling!

The Princess imagined the disappointed faces of everyone in Twinkleland Palace, Twinkletown and Fancy Pants if they returned without finding the Festive Fairies.

Then Unipiggle pricked up his ears. He'd heard the sound of a key turning...

The door opened just a sliver. A fairy in a little red hat poked his head out. "We aren't taking any more orders or expecting visitors!" he said wearily.

"Please go away!" And he shut the door again.

"No! Please wait..." called Princess Pea.

Unipiggle pulled the cord once more.

Ting-a-ling-a-ling!
Ting-a-ling-a-ling!

Unipiggle had learned that being loud and determined was usually best when he wanted something.

"Enough ringing!" came the voice from behind the door. The fairy sounded very huffy now. "There has been a big problem this year. You must leave!"

"Please can we come in?" pleaded Princess Pea, pressing her ear to the door. "Unipiggle and I are very good at solving problems. We might be able to **HELP** you — so much is at stake!"

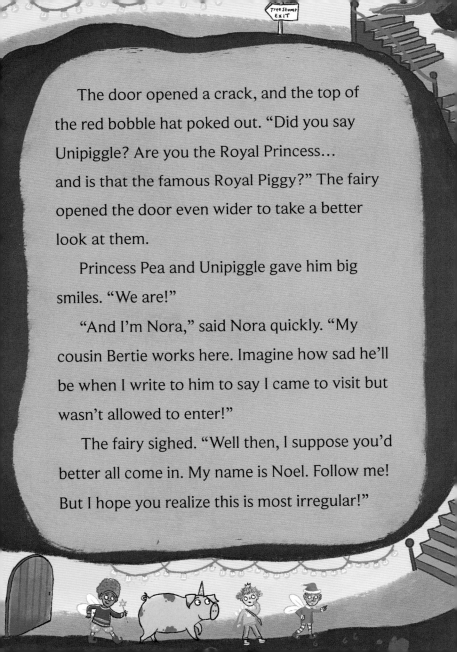

The door opened a crack, and the top of the red bobble hat poked out. "Did you say Unipiggle? Are you the Royal Princess... and is that the famous Royal Piggy?" The fairy opened the door even wider to take a better look at them.

Princess Pea and Unipiggle gave him big smiles. "We are!"

"And I'm Nora," said Nora quickly. "My cousin Bertie works here. Imagine how sad he'll be when I write to him to say I came to visit but wasn't allowed to enter!"

The fairy sighed. "Well then, I suppose you'd better all come in. My name is Noel. Follow me! But I hope you realize this is most irregular!"

Princess Pea, Unipiggle and Nora followed Noel up and down polished staircases and through winding tunnels under tree roots, before they emerged into a cavernous grotto.

"Wow!" gasped Princess Pea. "The Festive Fairy workshop!"

Unipiggle grunted in amazement.

The huge underground workshop was full of machines whirring away. Wrapping paper, ribbons and boxes were piled high, along with a jumble of gifts (some were distinctly pant-shaped). There were strings of fairy lights tangled in balls, decorations, labels, and piles of pine trees and wreaths. Long gift lists were

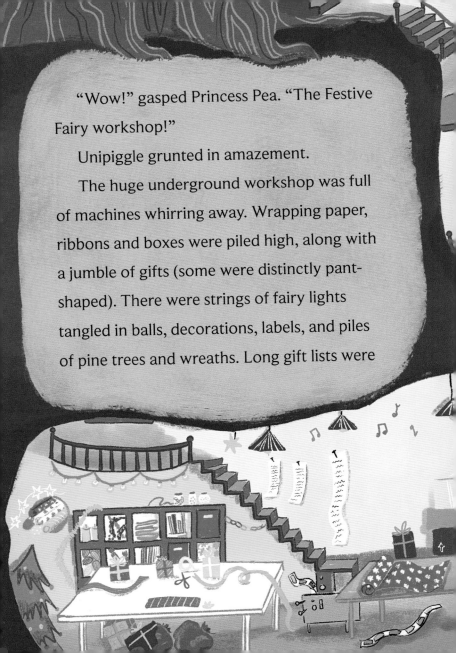

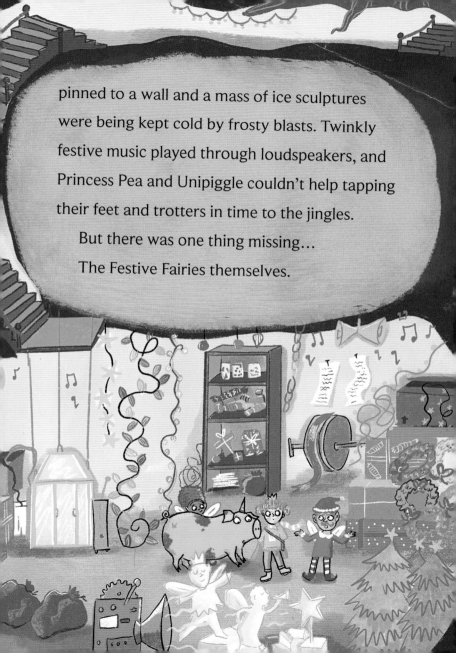

pinned to a wall and a mass of ice sculptures were being kept cold by frosty blasts. Twinkly festive music played through loudspeakers, and Princess Pea and Unipiggle couldn't help tapping their feet and trotters in time to the jingles.

But there was one thing missing…

The Festive Fairies themselves.

Festive Fail

"Where is everyone?" asked Princess Pea worriedly. Unipiggle sniffed around the abandoned ice sculptures, but there was no one to be seen. There really *was* a big problem.

"Through here," said grumpy Noel, opening a door to another underground chamber. There, sitting on toadstools, drinking cups of tea and looking very glum indeed, were lots of fairies. They were wearing matching little red hats and boots with bells on. They all turned to stare at the unexpected visitors, but no one smiled. A fairy who must have been Nora's cousin Bertie

waved sadly from a corner.

"What's wrong with everyone?" Princess Pea whispered to their guide.

"We're on strike," explained Noel. "That's why no one in Twinkleland has had their deliveries today."

"We've decided enough is enough!" piped up an even grumpier-looking fairy. "We work all day and night to get the festivities ready and bring sparkle and cheer to Twinkleland, but *we* don't get to enjoy winter or have festive fun ourselves…"

"And as soon as we're done, we have to start preparing for next winter!" squeaked Bertie, and he burst into tears. "We never stop! I don't think anyone appreciates us! What is snow even for?"

The little fairy blew his nose in a large hankie and Nora went over to comfort her cousin.

Unipiggle oinked softly and magicked some tea into chocolate to try and cheer Bertie up.

Princess Pea and Unipiggle exchanged worried glances. They hadn't realized how hard the fairies worked every year, or that they missed out on the festivities. It wasn't fair that they had to make all the gifts and decorations, but didn't get to take part in any of it. They had to show the fairies what having fun in the snow was like!

Luckily, Unipiggle had had the same idea and was already nudging fairies towards the door.

"It's a perfect plan, Unipiggle! Come on, fairies! Unipiggle and I are snow-fun experts. Come out with us and we'll show you."

Princess Pea and Unipiggle followed the fairies out through more tunnels and up some steps to a cleverly hidden secret exit in a tree stump. They were so glad that they could show the fairies how to play the snow games they'd learned, and even try out some new ones with them. The snow seemed much deeper here because they were still shrunk to fairy size. Unipiggle could only just poke his head above the surface in places; he felt like he was swimming in it! The Festive Fairies were soon giggling and rolling around, building snow castles, sledging and throwing tiny snowballs.

"To think, all this time we didn't know snow could be so much fun!" Bertie laughed as he and Nora made snow fairies together.

Feeling rather soggy, Princess Pea and
Unipiggle rested under a candy-cane tree
and watched the fairies play. Unipiggle gasped
as a large drip of water splashed onto his head.
Princess Pea looked up. The icicles were melting

and more puddles were forming. *Would it be hopeless if they tried to save the Snow Ball now?* One thing was for sure, she knew that Unipiggle wouldn't want to give up yet!

"Unipiggle, we can't stop the snow melting but we can do something about the festive deliveries. Let's sneak back into the workshop and finish what the Festive Fairies have started. We could make the deliveries ourselves! That way, the fairies could keep having fun, and we can make sure everyone else does too!"

Unipiggle jumped to his feet; he was ready to try.

"Let's do this!" Princess Pea beamed.

Happy Helpers

Princess Pea and Unipiggle busied themselves straight away in the workshop. There were still so many unwrapped gifts.

"I'll wrap and you pack!" Princess Pea told Unipiggle, who nodded and found some sacks. Princess Pea pulled out a huge roll of paper and some ribbons and set to work.

"Phew! This is **HARD** work!" Princess Pea wiped her brow as she wrapped what seemed to her like the hundredth gift (but was, in reality, only her fifth!). She handed it to Unipiggle, who

85

grunted and pushed it into a sack. Meanwhile, Nora had offered to help them too. She was printing out labels and trying to match them to the correct gifts, but it was tricky indeed.

"Have we only packed one sack?" she asked, checking the workshop clock. "We'll need to speed up for sure!"

Just then, the Festive Fairies flew back into the workshop. Their cheeks were glowing and their smiles were radiant. Princess Pea explained what they were doing. "Keep enjoying yourselves!" she urged. "We're taking care of everything and tomorrow you will all be invited to the Snow Ball as my extra-special guests!"

"You'll never do it all in time!" insisted Noel. He and the other fairies whispered between themselves. Then Noel turned back to Princess Pea and Unipiggle. "We're calling off the strike! There's too much joy to be had from bringing festive cheer to others — and with you helping and a Snow Ball to look forward to, it won't seem like such hard work!"

"Well…if you're really sure?" Princess Pea smiled gratefully. Unipiggle gave a thankful grunt.

With renewed energy, the Festive Fairies leaped into action. They nimbly wrapped presents at five times the speed Princess Pea could. They stuffed crackers, wound up fairy lights, checked off lists and printed labels.

Nora (while jotting things down in her notebook) helped Bertie add sparkle to the festive wreaths. Princess Pea polished ice

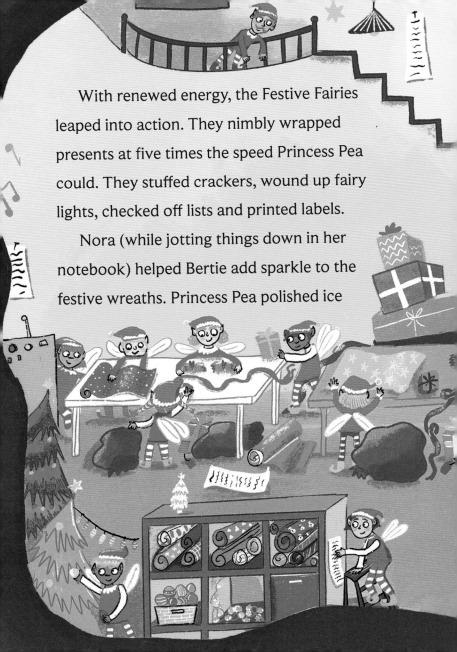

sculptures and Unipiggle tried to help tie bows on the last of the gifts. The fairies laughed like they'd never laughed before; gift wrapping was very funny with Unipiggle involved. The twinkly festive music was turned up loud and everyone bopped around the workshop, singing along and having a wonderful time.

A Twinkle-hour later, Noel pointed to the workshop clock. "We're almost ready! It's time to summon the reindeer!" he said. "Bertie, can you do that? Take our guest-helpers with you."

Unipiggle, Princess Pea and Nora looked keen; they couldn't wait to meet the magical flying reindeer. But Unipiggle and Princess Pea had begun to feel a bit odd… Princess Pea was sure she was taller than she had been a few minutes ago.

"Er…I think we should summon the reindeer straight away!" squeaked Nora, noticing Unipiggle beginning to expand quite rapidly. "Your candy-cane shrinking magic is wearing off!"

Special Deliveries

Feeling themselves growing bigger by the second, Princess Pea and Unipiggle hurried as fast as they could towards the secret exit with Nora ahead and Bertie fluttering anxiously behind them. They made it out just in time! (Well, almost — Unipiggle had to be pushed out quite firmly!)

Unipiggle rolled in a muddy snowy puddle to make himself feel better and then looked at Princess Pea. He was relieved to see they were both back to normal size.

The sky was full of stars and it was colder now.

"So how do we summon the reindeer?" Princess Pea shivered.

Bertie the Festive Fairy looked embarrassed. "This is my first time summoning them," he whispered. "Usually you need a trumpet, but I haven't brought it with me!"

Unipiggle grinned and Princess Pea laughed. "I know someone who can do extra-loud trumpeting without a trumpet," she said. "You'll need to hold your noses though!"

PAARRRRP!

The sound echoed around the glade, knocking icicles off the trees before drifting out into the Twinkleland night. Princess Pea, Unipiggle, Nora and Bertie waited (and held their breath too!).

Then... *Tinkle, tinkle*...

"I can hear bells!" whispered Princess Pea.

"Look!" said Nora, pointing at the sky.

A herd of reindeer appeared, pulling empty sleighs. Their antlers glowed with all the colours of the rainbow, just like Unipiggle's horn. They whizzed overhead a few times before landing silently and elegantly in the glade.

The reindeer lined up ready. They nodded politely to Unipiggle and he waved a trotter back.

"Wouldn't it be fantastic if Unipiggle could fly with them?" Princess Pea said to Bertie.

"He could! Their enchanted sleighs help them to fly," explained Bertie excitedly. "If Unipiggle wants to help pull one, he'd be most welcome!"

Unipiggle thought this was an excellent plan and went and stood in line with the reindeer.

Out came the other Festive Fairies, carrying bulging sacks of presents, which had magically grown to full-size, along with everything else they brought out. Princess Pea helped load it all into the sleighs. When everything was on board and strapped down, the fairies flew up to perch on the sacks. Nora and Princess Pea climbed into the sleigh pulled by Unipiggle.

"Dash away, all!" cried Noel, his fairy wand aglow.

With a whoosh of magic and Unipiggle's trotters racing, they took off — ready to help bring the festive cheer back to Twinkleland!

As they zoomed up into the night sky, Princess Pea looked down onto a moonlit Twinkleland below. Her heart sank a little as she saw how many bare patches of ground there were, where the snow had melted. She sighed. The Princess couldn't help feeling sad that the Snow Ball might not happen now, but they'd helped the Festive Fairies have fun and everyone would still be getting their deliveries to enjoy.

99

Then Unipiggle oinked as a single, cold snowflake whizzed past his snout. Princess Pea felt it land on her cheek. A moment later she felt another and Unipiggle squealed with joy as he spotted a flurry of flakes ahead.

"Hurrah! Unipiggle, it's snowing again!"

"Thank goodness!" said Nora.

"First stop, Fancy Pants!" announced Bertie as they prepared to land.

As the Fancy Pants villagers slept, Princess Pea and Unipiggle crept around the village and helped the Festive Fairies deliver gifts to every home. The biggest pants-shaped parcel was for the Mayor and the smallest was for Nora. She was delighted!

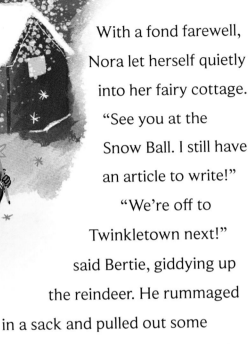

With a fond farewell, Nora let herself quietly into her fairy cottage. "See you at the Snow Ball. I still have an article to write!"

"We're off to Twinkletown next!" said Bertie, giddying up the reindeer. He rummaged in a sack and pulled out some interesting parcels, including a shiny new whisk tied up with ribbon.

"We know exactly who those are for, don't we, Unipiggle?" Princess Pea smiled. "After we've been to the bakery and brought cheer to

Twinkletown, we can head home!"

Unipiggle yawned in agreement.

And when they finally reached the palace,
they fell straight asleep. It had been a long and
adventurous day!

Goodnight,
darling!

Unipiggle woke with a start. He was in bed, and morning light was streaming in through the windows of Princess Pea's bedroom. He rolled off the bed and rushed to the balcony, pushing the doors open with his snout. Then he ran back and woke Princess Pea with a loud *"Oink!"*.

"There's enough snow outside for the Ball!" said Princess Pea joyfully. They peered over the balcony at the big pile of boxes that they had helped leave on the palace doorstep last night. "And it looks like the Festive Fairies have been too! I wonder if they have found the last-minute gift we left for *them* back at their workshop yet?" she mused and Unipiggle grinned.

"I do hope they like chocolate paperchains!"

105

9

Snow Ball

"This all looks wonderful," gushed the Queen, gliding past in a new winter gown. Arthur the Gardener Pixie was so shocked at getting praise from the Queen, he almost fell off his ladder.

"Careful, Arthur, you're nearly finished!" Princess Pea said. Unipiggle sat on the bottom rung to keep it steady. They'd been helping their pixie friend all morning, hanging the decorations and fairy lights they'd delivered up in the trees, while telling him about their adventures. The palace and gardens were looking twinkly, bright and festive; Princess Pea and Unipiggle couldn't wait for the Festive Fairies to come and enjoy it all with them.

"Have you read the *Twinkleland Times* this morning?" asked King Barry as he joined them.

The King was wearing a novelty festive crown and his moustache was spectacularly styled. He waved the newspaper at the Queen. "There's a gripping story all about the Festive Fairies and I bet you can't guess who else is in it..."

"Old news, Barry! Dearest Pea has already filled me in on the details. I sent off lots of extra invitations earlier to those poor fairy folk."

"The guests are already arriving!" Janet the Announcement Pixie and Bob the Trumpet Pixie informed everyone.

"Already!?" Arthur scrambled down the ladder and went off to change into his pixie partywear.

"Come on, Peasprout and Piggykins, we must meet and greet!"

They followed the King and Queen to the palace gates.

First to arrive was Baker Troll and his cat. The baker was carrying an awe-inspiring cake. It was shaped and decorated to look just like a miniature frosty Twinkleland Palace.

Other Twinkletown folk were helping him carry trays of sparkly, delicious-looking fairy cakes. "All healthy ingredients as usual!" he reassured the Queen.

More guests arrived and Princess Pea and Unipiggle were happy to see some familiar old friends. Next came the Fancy Pants villagers, resplendent in their lovely, shiny new pants. The Mayor laughed jollily and, much to their surprise, gave Queen Bee and King Barry a huge bear hug. Nora high-fived Princess Pea and Unipiggle, then headed straight to the banquet table, where she helped herself to a cake bigger than her own head.

"Time for some music!" declared King Barry, searching around for his ukulele...but it had

somehow mysteriously vanished. Princess Pea and Unipiggle shared a moment of relief; they hated the King's singing. The pixies quickly burst into song instead.

The party was just getting into full swing when a cheer rose up from the crowd.

"Look who's here!"

The Festive Fairies flew overhead in neat formation, while their reindeer flashed their rainbow antlers impressively. They landed on the parade lawn nearby.

"A warm welcome to our hard-working bringers of festive cheer!" declared the Queen. "We are lucky to have you — thank you for everything you do. From now on I will be sending royal help at snowfall every year!"

The Festive Fairies flew around, chatting excitedly, before they all headed to the ice rink to try out some skatey-slidey games. Unipiggle watched them from a safe distance; he'd had quite enough of ice this winter!

Princess Pea and Unipiggle had a dance, munched on a cake turret and played in the snow with their friends. They were so glad that everyone could enjoy the fun. As the final guests departed, they all agreed that the Snow Ball had been a great success.

"I almost forgot about gifts!" said the Queen, handing out parcels to everyone who lived in the palace.

"Oh…a new flannel," muttered the King. He'd hoped for a harmonica or maybe a kazoo.

It seemed that everyone had a flannel.

"There will be no excuses for grubbiness now! I even gifted myself one." The Queen smiled, feeling very pleased with herself. The Palace Pixies loved their flannels, but Unipiggle and Princess Pea sighed and tried not to look too ungrateful.

Princess Pea spotted another gift that hadn't been opened.

The King picked it up. "Ooh, is this for me?" He read the label aloud:

> *Dear Princess Pea and Unipiggle,*
> *Thank you for all the snowy fun!*
> *Please visit our workshop any time.*
> *Noel, Bertie and all the Festive Fairies*

Unipiggle tore off the paper and oinked with delight.

"A new sledge!" whooped Princess Pea.

"Very nice!" said the King, admiring its sleek red rails.

"But it will only be useful when there's snow," said the Queen. "Why, you'll be sledging on mud soon!"

Unipiggle and Princess Pea looked at each other and chuckled. Mud-sledging sounded like another brilliant adventure…

...In fact, such a brilliant adventure that they decided to try it straight away!

"Thank you, Festive Fairies!" yelled Princess Pea happily as they whizzed downhill.

Unipiggle oinked delightedly as he saw the Festive Fairies' sleighs and reindeer sparkle above them, loop-the-looping in the Twinkleland sky.

Princess Pea and Unipiggle's first ever Snow Ball together had been the **BEST**. They were definitely going to help out the Festive Fairies again next year (even if they weren't allowed to do any wrapping).

HOW TO DRAW A REINDEER

You will need: a pencil, a rubber and colouring pencils.

Step 1: Use a pencil to draw...

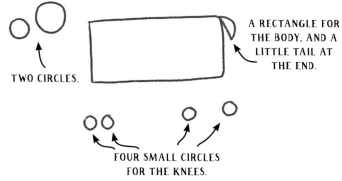

TWO CIRCLES.

A RECTANGLE FOR THE BODY, AND A LITTLE TAIL AT THE END.

FOUR SMALL CIRCLES FOR THE KNEES.

Step 2: Add details to your reindeer in pencil.

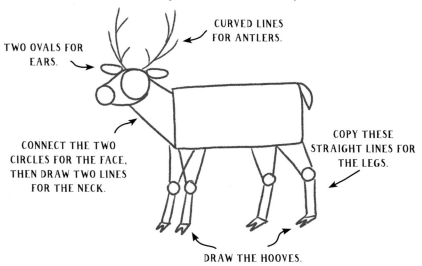

CURVED LINES FOR ANTLERS.

TWO OVALS FOR EARS.

CONNECT THE TWO CIRCLES FOR THE FACE, THEN DRAW TWO LINES FOR THE NECK.

COPY THESE STRAIGHT LINES FOR THE LEGS.

DRAW THE HOOVES.

Step 3: Use a coloured pencil to draw the outline of your reindeer on top of the pencil shapes.

DRAW ANTLERS AROUND THE LINES.

ADD TWO EYES, A NOSE AND A MOUTH.

ADD A COLLAR AND A LITTLE BELL.

Step 4: Rub out all of the pencil guide lines. Now it's time to colour in your reindeer, using your colouring pencils!

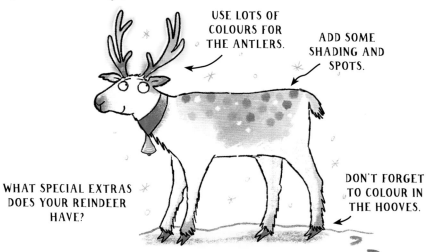

USE LOTS OF COLOURS FOR THE ANTLERS.

ADD SOME SHADING AND SPOTS.

WHAT SPECIAL EXTRAS DOES YOUR REINDEER HAVE?

DON'T FORGET TO COLOUR IN THE HOOVES.

SPOT THE DIFFERENCE

Can you find **FIVE** differences between these two pictures?